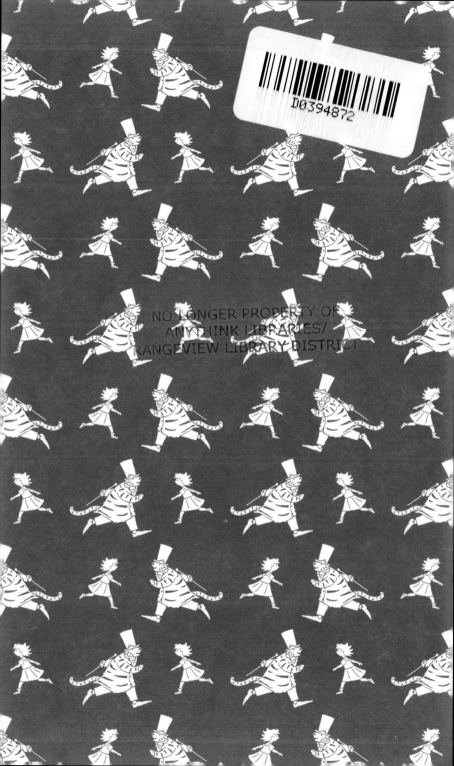

D03394872

# MR. TIGER,
# BETSY,
# and the
# BLUE MOON

PENGUIN WORKSHOP
An Imprint of Penguin Random House LLC, New York

Text copyright © 2018 by Sally Gardner.
Illustrations copyright © 2018 by Nick Maland.
All rights reserved. First published in the United Kingdom
in 2018 by Zephyr, an imprint of Head of Zeus Ltd.
Published in the United States in 2020 by Penguin Workshop,
an imprint of Penguin Random House LLC, New York.
PENGUIN and PENGUIN WORKSHOP are trademarks of
Penguin Books Ltd, and the W colophon is a registered
trademark of Penguin Random House LLC.
Printed in the USA.

Visit us online at www.penguinrandomhouse.com.

Library of Congress Cataloging-in-Publication Data is
available upon request.

ISBN 9780593095164          10 9 8 7 6 5 4 3 2 1

Typesetting & design by Jessie Price & Kayla Wasil

# MR. TIGER,
# BETSY,
# and the
# BLUE MOON

## Sally Gardner

### illustrated by
## Nick Maland

Penguin Workshop

*A* is from an island that has been left off the map of the world. It is the place where all the letters of the alphabet come from. And this is where our story begins. With a Mr. Tiger and a little girl called Betsy K. Glory and a rather large moon.

The letters of the alphabet had asked Mr. Tiger if he would like to help them write down this story. He was far too busy. The letters of the alphabet also asked Betsy. She said she was far too young. As for the moon, well, that would have just been plain silly, so it was left up to the letters of the alphabet themselves to tell the story. For there are more than enough letters to make every word ever needed. They decided that as *O* is the first letter of many a fairy tale, *O* should begin— with . . .

Once upon a time, there was a little girl called Betsy K. Glory. She had purple hair, bright, shiny green eyes, rosy cheeks, and a sweet, freckly face. Her mum, Myrtle, was a mermaid. Alas, she had not taken well to dry land and didn't have freckles.

Her father, Mr. Alfonso Glory, had done his very best to make his mermaid bride happy. But there is such a difference between sea and pavements, between having two feet and a mermaid's tail that, in the end, Betsy's dad and Betsy's mum both agreed to a parting of the waves. Betsy's mum went back to her home under the water. While Betsy, who didn't have a mermaid's tail, stayed on land with her dad.

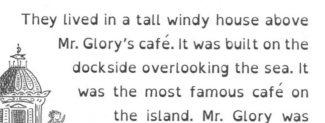

They lived in a tall windy house above Mr. Glory's café. It was built on the dockside overlooking the sea. It was the most famous café on the island. Mr. Glory was known for making the most wondrous ice creams. More delicious than any you have ever tasted. His crackle-galore flavors, his Chocolate Cream Wizards, his Ribble Raspberry Wonder were the stuff of dreams.

So famous was Mr. Glory's ice cream that people came from every corner of the island to eat there. Even though the island had been left off the map of the world, it hadn't stopped word spreading that Mr. Glory was the king of ice-cream makers.

Betsy lived a charmed life. The island was a peaceful place to grow up. It had sandy beaches, a blue ocean, and nothing horrible ever happened. Her mum often came to visit and on warm days they would go off swimming together in the sea.

We agree, it was somewhat sad that Betsy's mum couldn't live with them. In all honesty, it wasn't so sad that Betsy wasn't happy or she didn't feel loved. And although it would be good

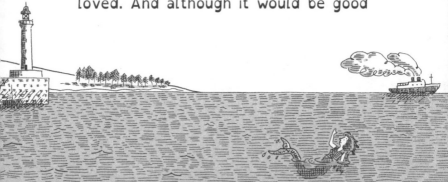

to always write stories that are about pleasant things, unfortunately, there would be very little to say. Except that the sun shone every day. That the rain rained every night and that Betsy's favorite day was Wednesday.

·← 2 →·

**B**ut, before we go any further, the letters of the alphabet want to say they were always busy. Not just writing this story. They were needed for all sorts of other important things, like the daily news. That is how Dad and Betsy first heard that Mr. Tiger and his circus were to arrive on Wednesday. But the trouble was, the letters of the alphabet weren't quite sure which Wednesday. Or more to the point, what kind of circus he would bring with him. Perhaps they didn't know because when Wednesday came, there was neither sight of Mr. Tiger nor sound of his circus.

Wednesday was the day Betsy's mum would pop out of the sea. Betsy would wait for her on the harbor steps and together they would dabble feet and fin in the water. That is, until Dad turned up to carry Mum back to his café. Here she would sit at one of the little tables, under a shady umbrella, with her tail in a bucket.

Betsy wondered if Mum knew anything about Mr. Tiger and his circus. But Mum had a faraway look in her eyes that had more to do with orcas and oceans than circuses.

"Do you think Mr. Tiger has animals?" asked Betsy. Before Mum could answer, Dad appeared with an ice cream he'd made especially for her. He had called it Myrtle's Minty Mumbo Marvel.

"It tastes of wishes," said Mum. "Delicious, mouthwatering wishes."

"What would you wish for, Mum?" asked Betsy. "If you had a wish."

Mum thought about this for a minute and said, "I have everything I could wish for—a beautiful daughter, a loving husband—what more could a mermaid want?"

"Legs," suggested Betsy.

Mum laughed. "Then I wouldn't be me, and you wouldn't be you."

"I hadn't thought of that," said Betsy.

"That's why," said Mum, "you have to be careful what you wish for."

Betsy asked her dad what he would wish for.

"Nothing," he said. "I have Mum and you. Anyway, a wish is very hard indeed to find."

Betsy wondered if there was a place where wishes were made. If there was, said Dad, he didn't know about it.

Mum knew of an island where Gongalong bushes grew. It was said that if the fruit was made into ice cream, you could make a wish from just one scoop and whatever you

wished for would come true.

"Then we should go there," said Betsy. "And we can pick Gongalong berries when they are ripe. Dad could make them into ice cream."

"Why," asked Mum, "would we need to do that when we have everything we want here on the seashore and in the tall windy house on the island left off the map of the world?"

"I just thought a spare wish might be useful."

Mum gave Betsy a hug. "But the island is as far away as Sunday," she said. "And I hear on the seaweed line that a bossy giantess rules it."

"That wouldn't stop Dad, would it?" said Betsy.

Dad was good at making ice cream but not so sure about giants, bossy or not.

"Wait a minnow," said Mum. "There

is something else important, but what it is I can't remember. It has something to do with how you pick the Gongalong berries."

She thought long and hard, but it had, for the present, swum away from her.

Later that day, as the sun was putting on its red pajamas and settling down for the night, Dad carried Mum back to the sea. He and Betsy waved farewell and watched as she disappeared beneath the white-kissed waves.

Betsy looked out of her window and up into a sweetshop of stars. There shone a white chocolate moon. She was about to climb back into bed when,

to her delight, she saw a star whiz across the black treacle sky. Closing her eyes, she said, "I wish Mr. Tiger and his circus would come tomorrow."

·← 3 →·

"Crumble cakes," said Betsy, for the next day, a ship had arrived in port. It was unlike any other she had seen before. Painted in blue and white stripes and festooned with flags. She wondered if her wish might have come true, without even one Gongalong berry.

Betsy went downstairs for breakfast and the first thing she wanted to know was if it was Mr. Tiger's ship. Dad was busy putting tubs of ice cream into the tricycle cooler. He was proud of his tricycle. It had been made especially so that he and Betsy could ride it together. On the side of the cooler, Mr. Glory had written the name of his latest creation: Myrtle's Minty Mumbo Marvel. And on the front was written: "Stop me if you want to buy one." It was this notice that made the going rather slow. Because wherever they went, they were always stopped. Especially when news spread that there was a new flavor to be tried.

The island, which had been left off the map of the world, wasn't very large. In fact, Dad and Betsy could cycle around it easily in a day. At lunchtime they would stop halfway up the tallest hill. In a field overlooking the harbor they would eat their picnic. Below, they could see the blue-and-white-striped ship festooned in flags.

"Do you think that it belongs to Mr. Tiger?" asked Betsy.

"Search my socks," said Dad. "If we were to start talking about tigers then we'd be here until moonrise and that would never do. When we're home

you can ask Mum, perhaps she might know."

The hardest part of the bike ride was pedaling up to the cave. It was on the steepest side of the hill. Here lived one of the ugliest toads you ever did spy. The toad was seated, as it always was, at the entrance to the cave, on a gray slimy stone.

Betsy would never go anywhere near it. So, it was Dad who would take out a tub of ice cream, open the lid, and then stand well back. They both watched as the toad flicked its long tongue into the ice cream. It would roll a scoop into its broad mouth, smile, and point to a gold coin.

"It's too much," Dad would say as he did every time they

visited the toad. But, as always, the toad would puff itself up as large as it could, which was the toad way of saying, "Worth that and more." Today being no different, Dad took the gold and climbed back onto the tricycle.

Then the toad who never spoke suddenly spoke!

"**T**his is probably the most delicious ice cream I have ever wrapped my tongue around," said the toad. "It tastes of wishes."

Dad and Betsy stared, openmouthed.

"You speak?" said Dad.

"Of course. Most princesses do."

"A princess?" said Betsy, as she dared to go a little closer.

"Yes, what did you think I was?"

"A toad," said Betsy.

"Is it really that bad?" asked the toad.

Betsy nodded. "Yes, I'm afraid it is."

"Oh dear, I still see myself as a princess with a rather long tongue. You don't happen to have a mirror?"

"No," said Dad.

"That's a pity," said the toad as she flicked out her tongue to take another helping of ice cream.

"This is wishable delicious," said the toad.

Betsy wasn't sure if it would be rude to ask how a princess had become a toad. Instead she said, "Why have you never spoken before?"

"I was lost for words," said the toad. "But now the Gongalongs desperately need my help."

"Oh," said Betsy. It didn't make sense that a Gongalong bush needed help.

"Goodbye," said Betsy, thinking it was perhaps best not to ask any more questions, if they were worth nothing more than silly answers.

"Are you going to leave just like that?" asked the toad. "Are you not an incy-wincy bit interested in why I am here, on this slimy stone?"

"Yes, of course we are," said Dad and Betsy together.

"Good," said the toad. "It is a very sad story. My half sister, Princess Olaf, believes that only a big person, with

big feet, can rule Gongalong Island and the Gongalong people. She has huge feet and shoes that need a lot of space. I, on the other hand, am the eldest and smallest princess. I only have tiny feet and tiny shoes. So she turned me into a toad."

While the toad was speaking, Betsy was sure she saw hundreds of glinting eyes, peeping out of the darkness of the cave.

"Can the spell be undone?" asked Dad.

"Yes, with a wish," said the toad. "All you need is to make ice cream from Gongalong berries."

"That is what I have heard," said Dad. "I could do that."

"No, you can't," said the toad.

"Although, thank you for offering. As I said, it is a very sad story, as the berries only grow when the moon is blue."

"When is there a blue moon?" asked Betsy.

"A very button-bright question, if I may say," said the toad. "They will not ripen under a pink moon. They will not ripen under a red moon. They will only ripen under a blue moon. But blue moons happen sometime never. And even when there is a blue moon you have hardly any time to pick the berries before the sun comes up."

Betsy let out a sigh. "Crumble cakes."

·+ 5 +·

Dad felt exhausted when he and Betsy returned to the café, but Betsy had as much energy as a jumping bean. She ran straight down to the sea. Mum had given her a shell that she could whisper into anytime she needed her. Betsy put the shell to her lips and waited. It always seemed to Betsy that Mum was never far away. For no sooner had she blown into the

shell than there she was.

Betsy couldn't wait to tell her about the toad. She was jammed full of questions. Where was Mr. Tiger? Who did the ship, festooned in flags, belong to? And the crown of all questions, when is a moon ever blue?

"Unfortunately," said Mum, "a blue moon happens sometime never."

"So that means," said Betsy, "Gongalong-berry ice cream is impossible to make."

"Unless," said Betsy's mum kindly, "you believe in magic."

Mermaids, Betsy thought, always were a little watery when it came to answering questions. Off she went to the harbormaster, who had a bushy beard, and asked if he had

seen anyone on board the ship. The harbormaster said he hadn't, for if he had seen Mr. Tiger, he would know. Mr. Tiger was quite unforgettable.

Betsy asked the lady in the flower shop, who didn't have a beard. She said she remembered seeing a ship like that in a glass bottle, bobbing up and down on cardboard waves.

The baker and the candlestick maker were both sure they had seen that ship when they were children.

But the butcher thought it was a load of rubbish. He didn't believe anyone had ever seen Mr. Tiger.

"He belongs to fairy stories," said the butcher.

It was, thought Betsy as she walked home, a mystery.

After tea that evening, Dad found a guidebook to Gongalong Island. In it was a recipe for Gongalong ice cream. The pages had turned yellow. Betsy loved the smell of old books. This one smelled of an island as far away as Sunday. In the middle of the book was a foldout map. It showed where the Gongalong berries grew but said they could only be harvested under a blue moon, which happened sometime

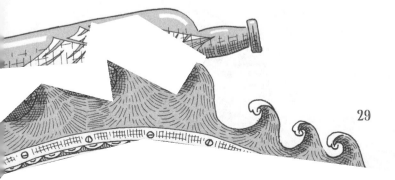

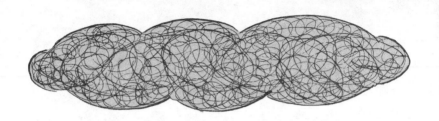

never. The *X* on the map marked
the spot where the berries could
be found. She turned the page and
there was a more detailed drawing of
a mountain. Underneath was written:
"The Mountain of Perpetual Mist."

"What does 'perpetual' mean?"
asked Betsy.

"It means mist that never goes
away. It is there forever and ever,"
replied Dad.

"Crumble cakes," said Betsy as she
continued to look through the book.

The guidebook said that the island
was the home of the Gongalong
people, who are even smaller than a
quarter of the size of your average

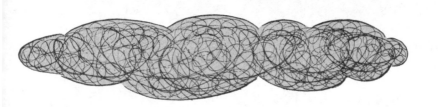

human being. They are as delicate as china cups and as strong as cement. Known far and wide for their amazing acrobatic skills.

"But it says nothing about the two princesses, not a word," said Betsy.

"It is an old guidebook," said Dad. "It might be out of date."

"What I don't understand," said Betsy, "is how the toad came here, from an island as far away as Sunday."

"Neither do I," said Dad.

"Also," said Betsy, "I don't understand who those glinting eyes belonged to."

"What eyes?" said Dad.

"The ones I saw in the cave behind the toad," said Betsy.

"Very odd indeed," said Dad.

That night, the lights on the blue-and-white-striped ship lit up. Yet still no one could be seen on board. Not until . . .

**⚹ 6 ⚹**

The following morning when Betsy looked out of her bedroom window, there in the distance she could see the top of a circus tent. She washed and dressed as fast as you could say, "frantic frogs fizzle on Fridays." She brushed her teeth, before sliding down the banisters of the tall windy house. Betsy landed, as she always did, in a heap at the foot of the stairs. Picking herself up, she ran to find Dad. Calling out all the while, "The circus has come to town!"

Dad was carrying a tray of breakfast things.

"Please let's go and see if Mr. Tiger is there," said Betsy.

"Why don't we eat first?" said Dad, handing Betsy a basket of freshly baked rolls.

"Do I have to?" she said as she followed him into the café. She was surprised to see, sitting in the corner, a gentleman reading a

newspaper. *That's odd*, thought Betsy, because the café was not open yet. But, stranger still, she caught a glimpse of an orange-

and-brown-striped tail beneath the table. She looked again. Those were not hands holding the newspaper, they were orange-and-brown-striped paws.

"Dad," said Betsy, as Mr. Glory put the tray down in front of the gentleman.

"Dad," she whispered. "Mr. Tiger!"

"Did someone say my name?" came a purring voice from behind the newspaper. Betsy could feel her legs go wobbly. There, seated in front of her, was none other than Mr. Tiger himself. He wore a smart top hat through which two furry ears stuck out, a bow tie, and a tiger skin coat, which was all his own. He stood up and towered over Dad and Betsy.

Putting out a paw, he said, "You must be Betsy K. Glory. A pleasure to meet you. Would you join me for breakfast?"

Betsy sat down and for the first time she could think of nothing to say.

"Alfonso was telling me you talked to the toad yesterday," purred Mr. Tiger.

Betsy nodded. She had never imagined that Dad actually knew him.

Finally, she found her tongue. "How long have you known my dad?" she asked.

"Now, let me think," said Mr. Tiger. He took out a pocket watch that had no numbers on it, just pictures. He studied it before he said, "Alfonso was about your age, eight years old. And then, of course, I was here when he opened his café. Not to mention being at his wedding to your mum, Myrtle. A wonderful day that was."

"You know Mum, too?" said Betsy.

"Yes, of course. And I came here to celebrate your birth."

"Why did you never tell me, Dad?"

But Mr. Tiger had other questions on his mind. "What did the toad tell you?"

Betsy told Mr. Tiger that the toad was really a princess, and that her sister, Princess Olaf, had put a spell on her.

Mr. Tiger let out a sigh that sounded more like a growl.

"We need to find a way to break the spell if the toad is to be saved," he said.

"What I want to know," said Dad, "is how the toad, I mean, princess, traveled here in the first place?"

"Simple—the cave," said Mr. Tiger. "It goes down beneath the sea, it twists and it turns, before it comes up on the side of the Mountain of Perpetual Mist."

"Then we are not a proper island," said Betsy.

"Very few islands are," said Mr. Tiger. "But the tunnel is no use to us, only teeny tiny people can use it. If we want to go to Gongalong Island, we will have to go by ship."

"Ship?" said Betsy. "The blue-and-white one in the harbor? Is it yours? Are we going with you?" she asked, jumping up and down.

"Well, I do hope so, as long as your

mum agrees to come, too,"
said Mr. Tiger.

*Sometimes happiness is
a red balloon*, thought Betsy.
*Round and big enough*

*to lift you off
your feet.*

"**C**rumble cakes," said Betsy when she saw Mr. Tiger's circus of acrobats. They were much, much smaller than her. Perfect in every way. They were shy and beautifully dressed. All their clothes were brightly colored. They had fancy stitching on their shoes and pointy hats.

"Morning, my gallant Gongalongs," said Mr. Tiger, addressing the acrobats. "There seem to be more of you than the last time I counted."

The acrobats nodded. "We would go

along with that," they said.

"Things have got so bad on the island," said one. "Many more of us are leaving by way of the tunnel."

"My gutsy friends," said Mr. Tiger. "This is terrible news, tell me more."

The acrobats made a Gongalong ladder, standing on one another's shoulders, and it was the last, highest acrobat who spoke to Mr. Tiger and Betsy.

"Princess Olaf has planted a hedge that has grown into a prickly, thorny fence. It goes

from one side of the island to the other. It has become near impossible to climb over and reach the cave."

"A fence?" said Mr. Tiger. "But that would be pointless, you are acrobats. A mere fence could not stop you."

The Gongalong spokesperson took off his hat, held it in his hands, and looked a sorry sight.

"The thorns are sharp," he said.

"This is far worse than even I thought," said Mr. Tiger.

"Far, far worse!" said the acrobats together.

"Princess Olaf knows about the secret tunnel. She suspects that's how her toad of a sister, the lovely Princess Albee, escaped," said the spokesperson.

"She guards the entrance in hope of snatching her if she should try to return."

"Why?" asked Betsy.

"So that she might steal the last wish from her. We can only escape when Princess Olaf is asleep."

"Did you say the toad, I mean, Princess Albee, has a wish?"

"They were each given three, but Princess Olaf stole two of Princess Albee's wishes."

"Then why doesn't she use the wish she has to be a princess again?"

"She can't," said the Gongalong spokesperson. "Only Princess Olaf can reverse that kind of wish, and she won't."

"Then there's nothing we can do," said Betsy.

"Yes, there is—a wish from some Gongalong-berry ice cream could make everything right as rain again."

"Excuse me. So do all the glinting eyes I saw in the cave belong to escaping Gongalongs?" asked Betsy.

"Yes," said the spokesperson.

"How did all this start?"

Mr. Tiger, who was superb at public speaking and liked nothing better than speeches, began to tell the story.

"Once the island of the Gongalongs was ruled by King Nudd. He was a kind king and much loved by his people. He had a daughter called Princess Albee. As pretty as a picture, as delicate as china cups, and as strong as cement. Seven years after the queen died, King Nudd married again. His new queen's distant relatives belonged to the realm

of the giants. The queen, though, was
as tiny as all Gongalong people are.
So, it was a terrible shock when their
daughter, Princess Olaf, started to
grow. In fact, she grew taller than her
mum, taller than her dad, and much,
much, much taller than her half sister.
But worse was to follow, little by little
her skin turned green with envy. For
she did not like the idea of sharing
anything one tiny bit. Especially not her
mum and dad, and especially not the
island. When the king and queen died,
she decided the only way of having the

island to herself was to turn her half sister into a toad.

"But enough," said Mr. Tiger, and from his paws came one sharp gold claw. "On to more cheerful matters. I wonder if Betsy might be allowed to watch our dress rehearsal for tonight's performance."

That afternoon, Betsy found herself seated next to Mr. Tiger. In a flick of a whisker she had forgotten about the toad as she sat, enchanted, watching the acrobats rehearse for the evening show. High at the top of the

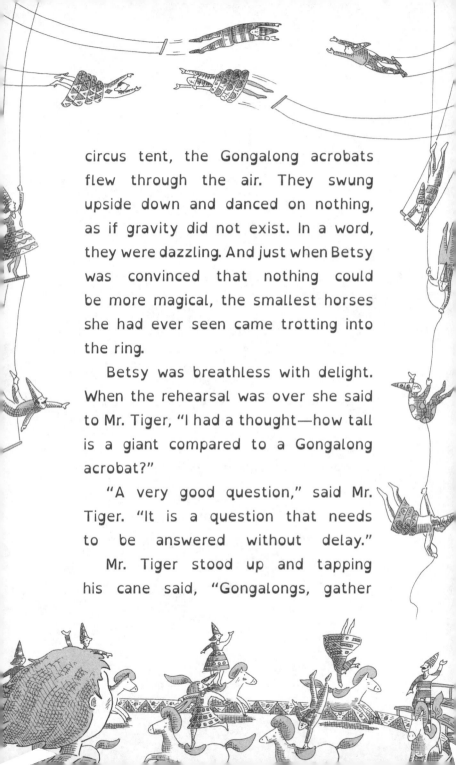

circus tent, the Gongalong acrobats flew through the air. They swung upside down and danced on nothing, as if gravity did not exist. In a word, they were dazzling. And just when Betsy was convinced that nothing could be more magical, the smallest horses she had ever seen came trotting into the ring.

Betsy was breathless with delight. When the rehearsal was over she said to Mr. Tiger, "I had a thought—how tall is a giant compared to a Gongalong acrobat?"

"A very good question," said Mr. Tiger. "It is a question that needs to be answered without delay."

Mr. Tiger stood up and tapping his cane said, "Gongalongs, gather round. Betsy K. Glory has a question."

Hundreds of acrobats appeared in the middle of the circus ring.

"Crumble cakes," said Betsy. "You want me to ask?"

"It is your question," said Mr. Tiger.

Betsy took a deep breath. "How tall is a giant?"

The acrobats huddled together and talked among themselves for what seemed like a long time.

"Begging your pardon," said the spokesperson. "You are a giant, Mr. Tiger."

"Am I as tall as Princess Olaf?" asked Mr. Tiger.

"No, she is taller. She is your height plus a Gongalong standing on top of your top hat."

Mr. Tiger clapped his paws. "Thank

you, my gutsy Gongalongs. Now, back to work."

"You know what this means," said Mr. Tiger to Betsy.

"Yes, Princess Olaf isn't as tall as we might have thought for a giantess."

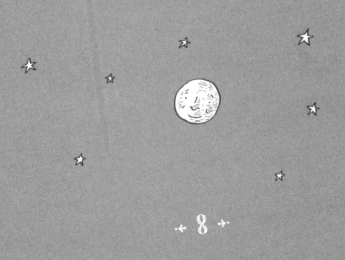

❖ 8 ❖

The rehearsal Betsy had seen was nothing compared to the magic of the show itself. That night, as the sun was setting and the moon was rising to take the best seat in the sky, the circus tent, festooned with flags, lit up with a funfair of fairy lights.

Mr. Glory had been busy all day making a new ice cream in celebration of the circus. Dressed in his striped jacket and hat, he handed out Hopscotch

Heaven. It was topped with a hundred gleaming colors that whizzed and sizzled on the tongue.

The band began to play as everyone took their seats, no one quite knowing what to expect. The drums rolled, the lights dimmed as Mr. Tiger prowled into the circus ring. He tapped his silver-topped cane and announced, "Ladies and gentlemen, for one night only we are here to amaze and delight you. To put starlight in your soul. To bring wizardry to your mind. Hope to your heart. Without further ado, let the show begin."

The audience gasped as the lights came up on the

Gongalong acrobats. That evening, Time lost all its power and Gravity lost all its weight. The acrobats, dressed in sparkling costumes, danced, whirled, and twirled through the air as if they had wings. The little horses galloped around and around as their riders performed daring tricks that thrilled, startled, and charmed. There was not a man, woman, or child who would ever forget the night they saw Mr. Tiger's circus.

In the morning, to everyone's surprise, Mr. Tiger and his circus had vanished. So too had the blue-and-white-striped ship. On the door of Mr. Alfonso Glory's café hung a notice. It read:

*Closed*

Everyone hoped that Myrtle might be able to explain where Mr. Glory and Betsy had disappeared to. But there was no mermaid to ask and even the toad's slimy stone was empty.

Happily, the sea was as flat as a paddling pool when the blue-and-white-striped ship set sail. It had pulled up anchor and disappeared without a sound while everyone in the town was fast asleep. Not even the harbormaster with his bushy beard had noticed its parting.

On board were Dad, Mum, Betsy, the

toad, and Mr. Tiger, of course. As well
as the acrobats. After all, who else
could sail the ship?

Betsy loved every moment of being
at sea. There was a swimming pool on
deck where Mum could bathe and the
toad could take a quick dip whenever
she wanted. There were so many things
for Betsy to take pictures of with her
camera and so many things to draw.
She watched the acrobats go up and
down the sails, keeping everything
shipshape.

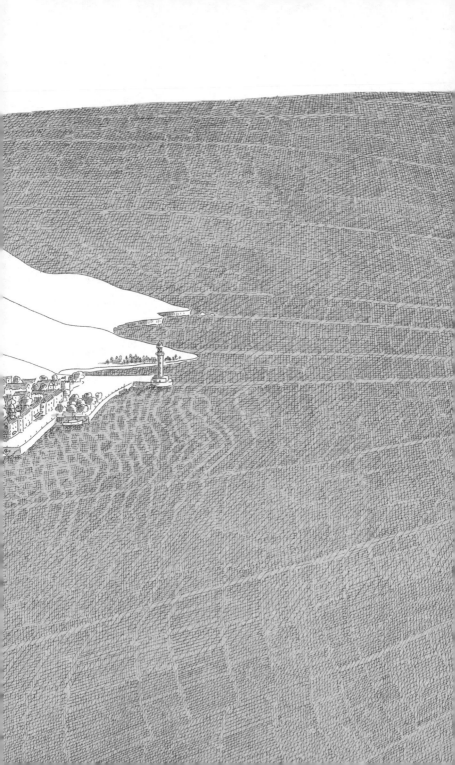

The first night, they were invited to
dine with Mr. Tiger. The meal had been
especially prepared by Mum's mermaid
friends from Fin's Fishery. Betsy, Dad,
Mum, Mr. Tiger, the toad, and as many
Gongalongs as could fit round the long

table all sat down to eat while the
silver moon shone and the band sang
songs of the sea. When the plates had
been cleared away and everyone had
thanked the mermaids, talk turned, as
talk often does, to the matter at hand.

What they were going to do when they reached Gongalong Island. The toad was worried about her half sister, Princess Olaf. She had threatened to turn her into a pie if she returned. Betsy worried about how they would ever make a silver moon blue.

Mr. Tiger took out his pocket watch and tapped the glass face with his golden claw, before saying, "We have a giant challenge, a moon to turn blue, berries to collect, and ice cream to create. Oh, and wishes to make come true. Worry not, my friends, I have a plan." Everybody asked what the plan was. He looked at his pocket watch again and said, "Cats have their secrets and their whiskers, their tales and their tails. In other words, the time is far from purrrfect."

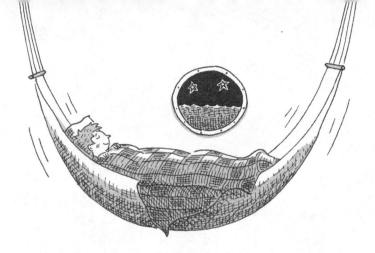

Later Betsy went to sleep in her cabin, snuggled up in her hammock. She was rocked gently back and forth on the rolling sea, feeling heartily happy. Dad lay in his cabin, wondering where on Gongalong Island he would find ice. Without it you cannot make ice cream. Not even if the moon did turn blue. It was a worry, thought Dad. And it worried him.

Now, some people are born worriers.
And some people don't worry at all.
And some people worry a little.
And wished they'd worried more.

·←· 9 ·→·

The sun was up and shining when Dad went to find Mr. Tiger in his cabin to tell him of his worries. Mr. Tiger told him that really there was no need to be concerned. The Mountain of Perpetual Mist was ice capped. It was easy. The acrobats could bring down buckets and buckets of ice.

Dad, being a worrier, thought it might be sensible to send word to the Gongalongs to check if that was

possible. A seagull took the message
and a seagull returned with the answer.
It read,

There is ice on top of the mountain . . .
But there are also shoes on top of the
mountain . . . Very big shoes . . . Scared
to go any further . . . So, no ice. Please
advise.
Signed, Kind regards, the Gongalongs

It was a strange message. What did
it mean? Mr. Tiger thought it most out
of keeping with the gutsy Gongalong
people. Dad thought it worrying. Mum

said that sadly she knew so little about mountains. Then the toad suddenly remembered what she had been trying to remember for as long as she had forgotten.

"I think," said the toad, "the shoes belong to the feet of Ivan the Timid."

"Who," said everyone together, "is Ivan the Timid?"

The toad tried her best to remember. Which only brought her out in lumps and bumps. She said that it was so long ago that she had forgotten. But she was sure that if she became a princess once more, all would be clear.

Betsy went to ask the acrobats if they knew anything about Ivan the Timid.

Sometimes if you ask the right questions, you get the right answers.

"Oh," they said. "We thought Mr.
Tiger knew about the legend of the
Mountain of Perpetual Mist. It is home
to a giant, but why he is there, nobody
knows. It would be doom and gloom
for us Gongalongs if he came down the
mountain. Although once he did send
a postcard but we couldn't read his

writing. The card was so big that it was used to make a house. He never wrote again, and that was the last we heard from him. He has become known ever since as Ivan the Timid."

Well, thought Dad, was it one worry less to know there was ice, even if a giant was sitting on it?

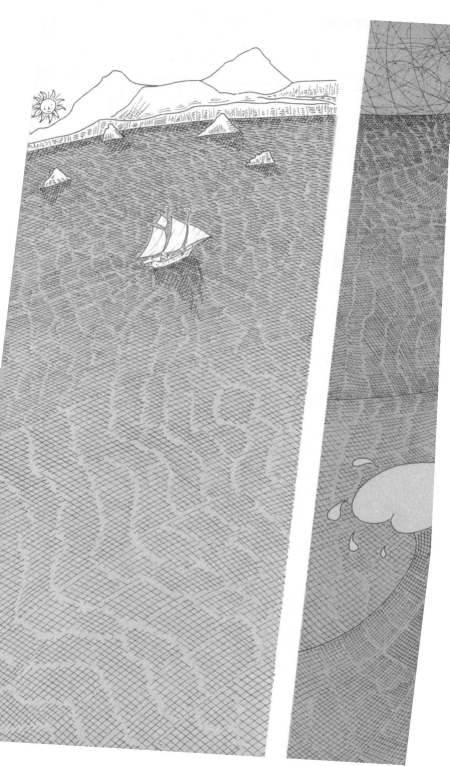

J ust when it felt as though the ship would never reach Gongalong Island and that they would be sailing to the end of all Sundays, the shout went up, "Land ahoy!"

"We are nearly home! We are nearly home!" sang the Gongalongs.

The ship dropped anchor on the north side of the island in a cove of pink seashells, well out of sight of Princess Olaf, who lived on the south, sunny side of the Mountain of Perpetual Mist. Mum wondered if it would be helpful if she went and spoke to the local mermaids to find out what was going on. Mr. Tiger agreed.

All day they waited for Mum to return, while the acrobats looked longingly at the shore. Even though they were very happy being with Mr. Tiger, they couldn't help wishing they were home. Mr. Tiger put his telescope to his eye and looked up at the Mountain of Perpetual

Mist. He gave a low growl.

Betsy asked him if he saw anything. But tigers are mysterious animals. Even if he had seen something, which Betsy suspected he had, it was not necessarily in a tiger's nature to say so.

At teatime, Mum returned. There was great excitement.

"What is the news?" asked the acrobats.

What Mum had to tell them was alarming. They could not sail to the south side of the island, as it was not safe. Princess Olaf was sitting at the mouth of the cave, tossing rocks into the sea. And that was not the worst of it. The fence had been built to give her the biggest part of the island. Where she now lived alone.

"What about our houses?" asked the acrobats. "What about our farms? What about our town?"

Mum shook her head and said, "I'm afraid Princess Olaf has big feet. She has left footprints of destruction everywhere."

"Oh dear, oh dear, oh dear," sobbed the acrobats.

"Oh dear," croaked the toad.

It was enough to put you off your tea. And all the whiz, pop, and sparkle seemed to have gone from the Gongalongs. They were very down in their cups and saucers.

Mr. Tiger brought out a map. "The fence doesn't stop us from climbing up the mountain," he said.

"No," said the acrobats.

"Then I think tomorrow we should pay a visit to Ivan the Timid."

The acrobats said, "He may call himself timid, but he is big enough to scare us. Remember the size of that postcard. It would be terrible if he came down the mountain."

"Can I go with you?" asked Betsy.

Mr. Tiger said that it was up to Alfonso and Myrtle to say whether their daughter could go or not.

"Oh dear," said Dad, who was always careful about everything he did. He didn't like the idea of his daughter going up a mountain. What if Ivan was a bad-tempered giant? What if he wasn't

as timid as everybody thought he was? More to the point, how would Betsy get up the mountain? After all, it was very tall and you couldn't even see how far up it went, because of the mist.

But Mum, who knew so little about mountains, thought it would be a good idea for Betsy to know more about them.

"I think she should go," she said, as she polished her tail.

Mr. Tiger said he would take Betsy up on his back.

"On your back," repeated Dad. "Is that safe? Surely Betsy should have a crash helmet? Oh dear, dear, this is very worrying indeed."

But once Mr. Tiger had demonstrated the safety features of his top hat, which was far more protective than any

normal crash helmet, on or off the map of the world, Mum and Dad agreed to Betsy's mountain-climbing adventure.

## ·← 11 →·

The sun had climbed out of bed hot and bothered when Mr. Tiger and Betsy set off the following morning. Betsy was wearing Mr. Tiger's top hat, and they were both eating kipper-paste sandwiches, as they rowed toward the pink seashell cove. A party of glum-looking Gongalongs greeted them. They were pleased to see Mr. Tiger, but did wonder if Betsy might be a giantess.

Mr. Tiger felt a speech was needed to cheer them up. He explained that, first, he was there to save the Gongalong people and to rid their island of Princess Olaf. Second, neither he nor Betsy were giants, and third, they wanted to climb the mountain and meet Ivan the Timid.

His speech didn't have quite the effect he thought it would.

"Best not to disturb him," the Gongalongs said, shaking their heads. "Look at the damage Princess Olaf has done and she has smaller shoes by far than Ivan the Timid."

Mr. Tiger was not the kind of cat to be put off so easily. With Betsy on his back, he set off up

the mountain, making light work of
the steep cliffs. In no time they had
reached the mist. Here they found
a battered sign, which read:

Home of Ivan the Timid,
53, Rockface,
Mountain of Perpetual Mist.
Please do not disturb
unless it is an emergency.

It was very, very cold up there and
Betsy was pleased that Mr. Tiger had
brought a warm coat for her to wear.
As the mist swirled it became harder to
follow the path. All they could hear was

heavy
breathing,
which
seemed to
make the mist
thicker, until it was
nearly impossible to
see where they were going.
Every now and again they heard an
odd sniffing sound or a sigh. Betsy
wondered if it was the wind. Mr. Tiger
said he doubted that. Suddenly he saw
a huge pair of shoes with a hole and a
toe poking out.

They looked up and up and, finally,
appearing out of the mist, was the
face of a somewhat woolly giant. Mr.
Tiger still had a packet of kipper-
paste sandwiches and he offered them
to Ivan, who timidly took one.

"My dear old top," said Mr. Tiger. "What are you doing up here all alone?"

"I am here to make sure," said Ivan the Timid, "that no giant ever walks or tramples over any of the little Gongalongs."

"Oh dear," said Betsy. "Haven't you heard about Princess Olaf?"

Ivan hadn't and was most upset when they told him. "This is terrible news," he said. "This is an emergency. I should have known, but the mist has become so thick these days that it's hard to see anything except a glimpse of the magnificent moon. I did send a postcard to the Gongalongs. I waited for a reply, but none came. Have you brought one?"

Betsy shook her head. "I'm afraid not."

"It's as I feared," said Ivan the Timid. "They are terrified of me."

"A misunderstanding, old top," said Mr. Tiger kindly.

"I've been awfully lonely up here with no one to talk to and not even a hot water bottle to keep me warm on winter nights. Sometimes I sing to the moon, but it doesn't notice me. Why should it?"

Ivan took another sandwich. He said kippers were his favorite, especially freshly caught kippers.

## ·+ 12 +·

"**L**oneliness," said Mr. Tiger, "is a terrible thing and it strikes me, old top, that you have been lonely for too long. The Gongalongs need your help as they have never needed it before. And I need your help if my plan is to succeed. We need to turn the moon blue so that we might make Gongalong-berry ice cream."

"You mean," said Ivan, "to make wishes come true?"

"Yes," said Betsy.

"The trouble is," said Ivan, "as I said, I would frighten the Gongalongs."

The giant had a point. His beard had grown so very long, his mustache had grown so very wide, and his fingernails had grown so very broad. Something had to be done.

"Would you ever consider, my old top," asked Mr. Tiger, "coming down from the mountain, going to the barbers, and having some new clothes? In short, being spruced up a little."

Ivan the Timid thought about this for a moment and said he would come down, as it was an emergency, but only if the Gongalongs wanted him to.

On hearing how lonely he had been and how unloved he felt, it was agreed something must be done. Mr. Tiger told

Ivan to wait until he heard their signal and only then to make his way down to the seashell cove.

"But what will the signal be?" called Ivan.

"A blast from the ship's horn," came a purr of a reply. And with that, Mr. Tiger and Betsy disappeared into the mist as fast as tiger paws can go.

It was so hot by the time they reached the bottom of the mountain that Betsy had to take off the coat she had been given by Mr. Tiger.

She wanted to ask if she could keep it but thought better of it. Mr. Tiger had a glint in his eyes, and from his paw she caught the flash of a gold claw. His mind was not on coats. Betsy

felt it would be a foolish question. Mr. Tiger gathered the Gongalong people together in the main square.

"My dear gutsy Gongalongs," he said. "There is indeed a giant sitting on top of the icy peaks of the mountain. He is big of build, chilly of fingers and toes that have outgrown his shoes. He is lonely of heart and longing to be useful. This, my dear Gongalongs, is a matter of a misunderstanding between a giant and yourselves. Ivan is a friend, not foe."

The minute they heard this, all the tailors on the island started snipping and cutting to make a suit big enough for a giant. It had to be patched together because there was not a length of fabric long enough.

The cobblers went to work on

making
comfortable
warm boots, soft enough
not to cause any damage to the
mountain or to the Gongalongs.

When everything was ready, Mr.
Tiger let out three hoots on the ship's
foghorn.

Ivan heard the sound through the
mist and, gathering his courage, he
made his way down the mountain.

To his surprise, the Gongalongs
were waiting for him.

The barbers and the manicurists
asked Ivan to sit on a rock
with his feet in
the sea. The
fish gave
him a

pedicure while the barbers, balancing on ladders, cut his hair. It was a bit like harvesting hay. They shaved off his whiskers, they trimmed his beard, and his nails were cut. Then they brought him more fresh kippers, his favorite, which are very hard to come by on top of a mountain.

Finally, he got dressed in his brand-new clothes. First, he put on a vest that the fishermen had made from their nets. Then a shirt of cozy brushed cotton. Pants and trousers, which were held up by braces. Next, a waistcoat with many pockets. Then a jacket with even more pockets, as a jacket without pockets is pointless. Then socks that had been specially knitted for him by sheep. Last, he put on his comfy boots.

He caught a glimpse of his reflection in the water and was so delighted with the way he looked that he posed for a picture.

"Smile," said Betsy, and he did. Because for the first time in a long, long while, he didn't feel so lonely and he knew he was loved.

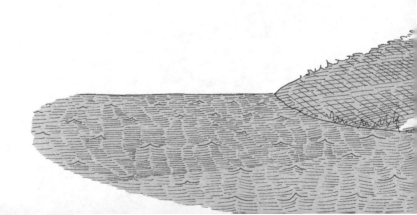

·←· **13** ·→·

Now that Ivan the Timid was no longer seated on top of the mountain, the snow-capped peaks could easily be seen from anywhere on the island. It was agreed that the cause of the mist must have been the giant's breath. For since he had come down, the sky had cleared.

Mr. Tiger could not have been more delighted with the outcome. From the ship, he could easily take the measurements he needed between the mountain and the moon. These he wrote down in his notebook. Then he would take out his pocket watch and study it carefully before saying, "Purrrfect."

Betsy often wondered what kind of pocket watch it might be. Especially as there were no numbers on the face to tell the time. Only the occasional picture, which appeared in a heartbeat and vanished in a second. Betsy asked Mr. Tiger if he would explain its workings. He just said, "Cats have their secrets and their whiskers, their tales and their tails."

Then one morning after breakfast, a picture popped up on his pocket watch of such importance he called everyone together in his cabin. He tapped his silver-topped cane and said, "My gutsy Gongalongs, gather round. Tomorrow, by my reckoning, there will be a full moon. This is the moment we have all waited for. It is our only chance of sometime never to turn a silver moon blue."

Betsy wasn't alone in wondering how such an impossible thing could be done. Dad and Mum were also confused. Neither Mr. Tiger nor the acrobats would say any more on the matter, apart from that tomorrow was going to be the night of all nights.

The acrobats had been busy for days, taking the things needed from the ship, such as ladders, wires, and ropes, to a camp they had set up at the

top of the mountain. It had not been easy work, on account of Princess Olaf. She stood on a stool, glaring over her fence. The minute she saw a Gongalong, she would shout, "I built this fence to keep you out. This is my island. Mine, not yours, never yours, just mine!"

When no one took any notice of her, she began to throw rocks to frighten the Gongalongs away. And, although the acrobats were quick on their feet, it did nonetheless make their task that bit harder.

It puzzled Betsy greatly as to

why one sister was so different from the other. She went and asked the toad if she knew the answer to this troublesome question. The toad, who had been too frightened to leave the ship in fear and trembling of Princess Olaf, agreed it was a puzzle.

"Do you know the answer?" asked Betsy.

The toad said, "I think it's a case of too many yeses."

"What does that mean?" asked Betsy.

"Simple when you think about it,"

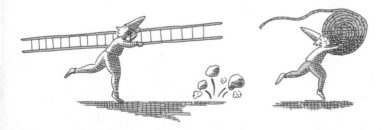

said the toad. "A 'yes' means yes and a 'no' means no."

"Sorry," said Betsy. "I still don't understand."

"That's because you are not spoiled," said the toad. "You see, all the yeses in the world makes no one happy. Not even a princess. It is the word 'no' that makes the word 'yes' all the more special. Because without a 'no,' you never realize how lucky you truly are."

"I hadn't thought of it like that," replied Betsy.

"Why should you?" asked the toad. "I'm the one who's been sitting on a slimy stone for years with nothing to do but think. I could do with a tub of ice cream to settle my nerves. Your dad isn't, by any chance, making ice cream today?"

"No," said Betsy. "We are waiting for the moon."

"Of course," said the toad. "Silly me, it really doesn't matter."

There was one thing left on Mr. Tiger's list. That was for the acrobats to take the sea-blue circus tent up to the camp at the top of the mountain.

"Once that is done," announced Mr. Tiger, "we will be ready. Alfonso, you need to take your ice-cream equipment to the island and have everything in place for when the Gongalong berries are harvested."

"Please don't forget that I need buckets of ice to make the ice cream with," Dad said.

Mr. Tiger licked the top of his pencil and his whiskers. "Of course. The acrobats will bring buckets of ice down with them. Then all will be as peachy as only paws and claws can be."

While this was going on, Betsy had been busy studying the map of the island, which was spread out on the table in Mr. Tiger's cabin. There was, she thought, a rather big problem that Mr. Tiger may have overlooked.

"Excuse me," she said, "but have you forgotten that the Gongalong bushes are on Princess Olaf's side of the fence?"

"Quite so,"
said Mr. Tiger
with a swish of his
tail. "I have a plan up my sleeve for
that!" He was about to explain what
his plan was, when one of the acrobats
somersaulted into the cabin. The
Gongalong stood up, took off his hat,
and said he was sorry, but he had come
to report that the circus tent had gone
missing. They had looked everywhere.
And at last they had
found it.

"Where?"
asked Mr. Tiger.

"That is the bad bit of the news,"
said the acrobat. "The circus tent is
wrapped around Princess Olaf. We
think she had grown bored of sitting at
the mouth of the cave, especially after

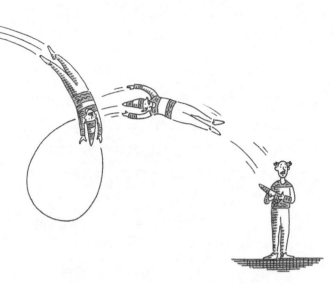

she had seen the circus tent. She is using it as a cloak. The silk trails over the town hall, through our streets, and nearly out to sea. We don't know how to get it back."

"This emergency is not on my list," said Mr. Tiger, letting out a loud and fearsome growl. "This is where we need the help of Ivan the Timid."

Ivan the Timid was, that morning, to be found paddling in the sea, helping the Gongalong fishermen catch fish. He had his trousers rolled up and was the happiest he had been in a long, long, long time. It had never occurred to him that he could be so useful, or that the Gongalongs would be so pleased to have a giant as a friend. But when Mr. Tiger told him what had happened to the circus tent, his knees started to shake, making waves that caused the fishermen's boats to bob up and down.

"This, old top," said Mr. Tiger, "is an emergency if ever there was one. We need you to bring us back the circus tent. And to make sure that we have a clear path to the Gongalong bushes."

"Oh dear," said Ivan the Timid. "You see, the trouble is, my name includes the word 'timid.' A timid person could never do the things you've asked. Perhaps if you could find another

word to describe me? Possibly that might help me to be more up to the challenge."

Mr. Tiger went back to his cabin and came out with a box of thinking caps that he kept especially for emergencies like this. He handed them out to Betsy, Dad, Mum, and, of course, the toad, as well as Ivan the Timid.

"These help," he said, "to think about words and their meanings. We need a new word that will give Ivan strength."

Everyone thought very hard. Ivan the Timid came up with "fearful," but then said timidly that he really meant "fearless." The toad came up with "glorious," which had more to do with

ice cream than anything else. Dad came up with "daring." Mum came up with "courageous." Mr. Tiger came up with "brave." Betsy came up with "bold."

"Ivan the Bold. That's it!" they said together.

Ivan sat on a rock. He dried his feet and put on his sheep-knitted socks and boots. "Bold tops timid," said Ivan and he stood up proudly.

The anxious faces of the Gongalongs looked at him. "You can do this," they said. "You can, we know you can."

"I can do this," repeated Ivan. "After all, I am now Ivan the Bold."

"Crumble cakes," said Betsy. "That word really suits you."

"Here I go, then," said Ivan the Bold, straightening out his jacket. The Gongalongs gathered to wave him off. But Ivan the Bold didn't move.

"Perhaps," he said, "I should take some flowers, a peace offering for Princess Olaf?"

"A good idea, my old top," said Mr. Tiger.

In a little while, quite a bunch of flowers had been picked and tied up with string. But still Ivan the Bold just stood, not moving.

"What's the matter now?" asked Betsy. "Why aren't you off?"

"I am thinking," said Ivan the Bold. "I am thinking that I need a plan and that my plan needs a small box and that my small box needs holes."

A small box with holes was found. The Gongalongs waved goodbye and shouted good luck.

Ivan the Bold walked toward the fence humming a bold sort of tune. The sort of tune he hoped would let a princess know that a giant was coming to say hello.

## ·← 16 →·

**P**rincess Olaf was swamped in the blue circus tent. It was so huge that it made it difficult for her to move. On her head she wore a crown of red rubies. She made a colorful sight, what with the blue of the circus tent, the green of her skin, the red of her crown. And there she sat, on top of the Gongalong town hall, busily rewriting the history of the island.

She wanted to make absolutely sure

that her half sister, Princess Albee, was never mentioned in any of the history books. It was to be known by one and all that she was the only princess who mattered. She had been left six wishes. She crossed that out and wrote "five," as she had failed to steal the last wish from her toad of a half sister. But once she caught her, she would be able to say six wishes. It didn't matter a fig or a parsnip to Princess Olaf that she had stolen wishes that weren't hers. Six is a lot of wishes for anyone to have. They should always be used wisely, for even one wish is hard to come by, let alone five.

The first thing Princess Olaf had wished was to turn her half sister into a toad. And to make double sure

it stuck, she had used two wishes. The third thing she wished for was an everlasting pot to be filled with whatever food she felt like. Except she had dropped the pot into the sea because it was too hot. The fourth wish had been to make a fence grow with the sharpest of thorns.

Now she had just one wish left.

She wondered if it wouldn't have been better if she had used her first two wishes to wish that she never ever had a sister. *Yes*, she thought, *I should have wished for that instead of turning her into a toad.* She picked up her pen . . .

Except we, the letters of the alphabet, refused to take part in her

lie. After all, every Gongalong worth its acrobatic socks knows that there are two princesses, not one.

Princess Olaf sniffed the air and then sniffed the air again.

"Dragon bums," she said out loud. "My toad of a sister is not far away,

I knew it! I knew it!"

Then she saw Ivan the Bold step over her fence, as if it were made of

nothing more than dandelion clocks.

"Go away," she said.

"Hello, I am Ivan and I have brought you some flowers."

Princess Olaf began to laugh. "You are Ivan the Timid, you just sat on top of the mountain, in a perpetual mist of

your own breath. Spare me! Go away! I am bored by you already."

"These days I am known as Ivan the

Bold and I have come to ask," said Ivan politely, "if you will take down the fence?"

"No, never," said Princess Olaf. "And don't ask me to change back my half sister, because I won't. She is a toad and a toad she will stay."

"You aren't even a proper giant," said Ivan.

"I am. What makes you say that?"

"You are a bit on the small side."

"I am not," shouted Princess Olaf and she stamped her foot so hard that the rocks began to rumble.

"If you were a proper giant," said Ivan, "you would be able to touch the sky and bring down a cloud."

Princess Olaf looked at the sky. The clouds were very far away. "No one can do that, not even a giant," she said.

## 17

I van the Bold pulled down a fluffy white cloud and handed it to Princess Olaf.

"That proves nothing," she said angrily, and she stamped on the cloud and the flowers as well. "It is not size that matters. I am by far a greater giantess than you will ever be." She crossed her arms and said, "I bet you can't . . ." and then thought for a moment, "I bet you can't . . . can't . . ."

"Make myself any bigger?" suggested Ivan.

"No," she said. "Make yourself as small as a . . ."

"Frog," said Ivan helpfully.

"All right," said Princess Olaf. "I command you to make yourself as small as a frog."

"I can't do that," said Ivan the Bold, "because I am just a giant."

"I could," said Princess Olaf. "It is easy."

"I don't believe you," said Ivan the Bold. "I don't know any giant who could make themselves that small."

"That's because you don't know any proper giants. You've been stuck up on top of a mountain, spending your days making mist. I will show you," she said, and she closed her eyes and mumbled,

"I wish to be a frog."

"Still doesn't prove you're a giant," said Ivan the Bold. "Just a fool for using up the last of your wishes."

"Turn me back! I wish to be turned back. I command you to turn me back now," shouted Princess Olaf the frog.

"Whoops," said Ivan the Bold. "I can't do that."

Princess Olaf tried to hop away but

Ivan quickly bent down and scooped up the green and purple frog. He put it in the small box with holes in it, making sure the lid was tight. After that he folded the circus tent neatly. He took off his boots, rolled up his trousers, and waded into the sea, where Myrtle was waiting for him. She took the box and, after putting it in an airtight bag, swam away to find a certain ship whose captain had a great interest in amphibians. That is the study of frogs and toads, to you and me.

## 18

Meanwhile, the Gongalong people waited breathlessly for Ivan's return. The hopes of the island rested on the giant's shoulders. Hours passed, by which time the sun was tired of throwing its golden ball across the sky. There was still no sign of Ivan the Bold. Mr. Tiger kept an amber eye on his pocket watch and said nothing. Dad was too busy to think about it, which was a good thing. Otherwise he would have worried a lot.

Betsy sat calmly and looked at the fence. "Bold," she thought, was a cracking word, a strong word. "Bold" was not a word that would let you down.

"What will we do if Ivan the Bold never comes back?" said the Gongalongs. "What will we do if Princess Olaf has turned him into a . . ."

"No, don't say it," said the toad.

Just when they feared that all was lost, as lost as lost could be, Ivan the Bold came boldly back. He was

draped in the circus tent and had spent the afternoon pulling up the fences that divided the island.

Everybody cheered and clapped when they saw him and shouted, "Speech!"

Ivan went a bit red. "It matters little what size you are," he said. "What matters most is how you feel inside, and I feel mighty bold, I can promise you. You will never be bothered by Princess Olaf again."

"Hooray, hooray," said the Gongalongs, throwing their hats into the air. Which was their way of saying they were pleased as pleased could be.

Ivan the Bold said, "Wait, first we need to clean the circus tent, as Princess Olaf has dragged it through the mud. It looks a little less blue."

Fortunately, the mermaids came to the rescue, which was a good thing because the sun had begun to sink sleepily from the sky in search of its bedroom on the horizon. The mermaids took the circus tent out into the deepest sea where the waves roared

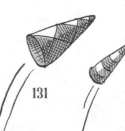

stronger than a washing machine. There it tumbled and rolled until it was bluer than the sea itself.

The evening breeze blew its warm breath until the silk was dry and ready.

## ·+ 19 +·

Dad had been given a very old leaflet by the mayor. It was: *An Instruction Manual for the Gongalong Berry Picker in the Unlikely Event of a Blue Moon*. There were only three instructions and they had been handwritten:

1. Never pick a berry. Wait, only ripe when in flight.

2. Never, ever forget a butterfly net.

3. Sunglasses a must for the eyes, unless you want a nasty surprise.

"What does it mean?" Dad asked the mayor.

The mayor shrugged and said, "We have scholars who've made it their lifetime's work to study these three facts."

"And," said Dad hopefully, "did they come up with any answers?"

"No," said the mayor, "but they found out the meaning of the word 'blue.'"

It occurred to Dad that even if a berry could be grown, that would not mean the end of the problem. Far from it.

Now here, we, the letters of the alphabet, feel we should say a word or two about Mr. Alfonso Glory, because we know perfectly well that Mr. Glory won't.

He was brilliant at making ice creams
and also at inventing things, so that's
what he did. He went to work inventing

a machine that would make sure not one berry went to waste.

It was an extraordinary-looking thing and would have been finished sooner, if it wasn't for all the questions the Gongalongs had to ask. These meant Dad often had to stop what he was doing and try to explain.

"This is my latest invention
It's made from an um
Which is found in an engine
With part of a drum
And a chain from my bike
Stuck together with
Sharp nails and a spike
And a vacuum too
To catch the berries when ripe
To make wishes come true
It's an ice-cream machine
To be put to the test
One that has never been seen
And I hope it's the best."


"Will it work?" asked Betsy.

"That's like asking," said Dad, "if
the moon will turn blue."

Mr. Tiger came to inspect it. He
glanced at his pocket watch and said,

"Alfonso, you have created the right machine for the right situation."

"You really think so?" said Dad.

Mr. Tiger put a paw on Dad's shoulder. "No point in worrying. What will be will be, you'll see."

Mr. Tiger ticked off the last thing on his long list, the circus tent, which had now been delivered safely to the top of the mountain.

No one, not even the seagulls, felt sleepy that night as the sun climbed under its red blanket.

The moon was wondering what was going on. It had never seen a giant sitting on top of the Mountain of Perpetual Mist before.

It looked at the giant and thought, *He has a face not unlike mine. Round, wise, and pale. I wonder if he is as lonely as I sometimes feel up in my night sky? The sun always turns its back on me. Never lets me play in its games and rarely even bothers with good morning or good night.* The moon went a little closer. In the silvery light, next to the giant, was a neatly folded blue circus tent. Now, there was nothing that the moon liked better than a good circus, especially if that circus belonged to Mr. Tiger. It went closer still and, to its surprise, saw Ivan the Bold holding up a mighty tall ladder.

*What is he doing?* thought the moon.

It felt the ladder resting on its round roundness.

"Good evening," said the moon.

Ivan looked up. "Good evening, Moon."

"What are you doing up here on the mountain with your ladder resting on me?"

"What are you doing, Moon, coming so close to Gongalong Island that my ladder can rest on you?" said Ivan. "I have never seen you so close and shining as silver bright as you are tonight."

"I wanted to see if Mr. Tiger is performing another of his amazing shows."

"And we were hoping to turn you blue so that we might pick Gongalong berries."

"You mean to make wishes come true?"

"Yes," said Ivan the Bold.

"And how were you going to do that?" asked the moon.

"We hoped by hanging the circus tent over you. A blue circus tent," he added.

"I think," said the moon, "that a circus tent is a bit on the small side."

It was true. The moon was vast and round and so close now that the ladder reached it with no trouble at all.

It was then that the moon spied the acrobats as they gingerly climbed up the ladder and tiptoed onto its ticklish surface.

"Are those Gongalong acrobats climbing onto me with their little horses?"

"Yes," said Ivan.

"Let me think what can be done," said the moon. And it disappeared behind a cloud, leaving Ivan holding the ladder. Ivan was very pleased when he felt the moon return.

"After the show is over," said the moon, "I might be able to climb higher still into the night sky and by doing so become smaller. Still, I think even then your circus tent will not cover half of me, perhaps not even a third of me."

"It would be worth a go," said Ivan the Bold. "And I am sure Mr. Tiger would be honored to have his circus

perform for you. Whatever you could do we would be most grateful."

Before the moon could say "jump," "cow," or "spoon," the acrobats had already landed and all the little horses began to prance.

"Is Mr. Tiger coming with the girl with purple hair, by chance?"

Ivan nodded. "They are waiting down here with me."

"Then send them up," said the moon. It shone brighter as it noticed Mr. Tiger was carrying a box, which he handed to Betsy. What was in the box, the moon could not see.

"Please don't move, Moon," said Ivan. "They are on their way up now."

"I won't," said the moon.

Ivan held the ladder for Mr. Tiger, with Betsy sitting on his back, clinging

tight to her top hat and the box, which wasn't easy. Mr. Tiger climbed up the rungs with the swiftest of tiger paws, until they had safely landed on the moon. By which time the acrobats had hung the circus tent from one crater to another. But, alas, it was more like a picnic blanket than anything that would turn the moon blue.

"Leave the flag," said the moon. "That belongs to the last fellow who was up here. Not very friendly. He wore a huge space suit and never once asked if it was all right to stick a sharp flag into me.

"Should I close my eyes until you are quite ready to begin?"
"A good idea," said Mr. Tiger.

## ·← 21 →·

This was such a momentous moment that Mr. Tiger felt a speech was needed. He tapped his silver-topped cane and bowed. "Oh, Moon of Muchness that shines on Gongalong Island, this is an honor indeed for a tiger of secrets and whiskers, tales and tails, to present a spectacle that is out of this world. Performed by the many feet of magical Gongalong acrobats and their horses."

"Wait!" interrupted the moon. "Are you about to say, one small step for a Gongalong and one mighty step for tiger paws?"

"Indeed not," said Mr. Tiger. "Why?"

"Only that is what the space man said. It gives me the shivers to think of those clumsy space boots clambering all over me," said the moon.

"I wouldn't dream of such a thing," said Mr. Tiger. "Shall we begin?"

With a tap of Mr. Tiger's cane, the musicians started up and the show began. First, huge hula-hoops of light, with the acrobats spread-eagled inside, whirled across the top of the moon. On wires that ran from star to star, they bicycled back and forth. Sometimes they stood on one another's shoulders, twenty Gongalongs high. The little

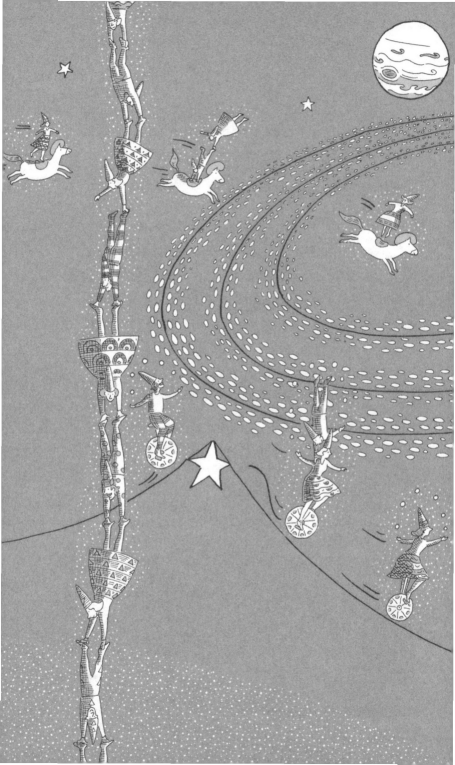

horses galloped and flew over craters. The acrobats, shimmering and twinkling with moon dust, whirled and twirled as if they were made from the air itself. On the moon, gravity made their bones weightless and their hearts happy. Nothing was impossible. They whizzed round and round and as good as flew through the air on their little horses. They rolled and tumbled until the moon was giddy beyond boundless.

"Oh," said the moon. "Oh, the muchness."

After the show was over, the acrobats climbed carefully down the ladder, taking their horses with them. Only Mr. Tiger and Betsy were left to say goodbye.

The moon shone more silver than it had done in trillions of

light-years, which was its way of saying thank you.

"This is sad," said the moon. "I hate to see you go. It makes me feel like waxing. It makes me want to wane. But for all that I have an honest light and I need to tell you that no matter how high in the sky I might rise, your circus tent is never going to be big enough to turn me blue."

"With great respect, Moon," said Mr. Tiger, "I thought you would say that. I have a plan. With the help of our dear friend in the box, there may be a remedy."

Betsy opened the box.

The moon was curious. "What is in there?"

"A toad," said Mr. Tiger as Betsy carefully lifted the toad out.

"Remember," she said, "what you have to wish for."

"Don't be silly, how could I forget?" said the toad. She puffed herself up.

"I wish with all my might to make the moon shine blue and bright,

By making the circus tent big enough to cover it tonight," she croaked.

It wasn't a good rhyme. Betsy thought it was quite embarrassing and wondered if a bad rhyme might make

a wish go wrong. She need not have worried, because the circus tent began to grow. It draped itself over moon rivers, moon mountains, and moon marshes until the moon's surface was completely covered and its silvery light shone blue through the silk of the circus tent.

"Well, I never," mumbled the moon.

It was hard to speak under so much fabric.

Mr. Tiger thanked the moon for being so understanding and promised they would visit, if the moon ever chose to come this close to Gongalong Island again.

"Oh dear," said the moon. "Seeing you go makes me blue, bluer than a blue should ever be. I'm probably bluer now under the circus tent than I have ever been before. Blue enough to pop a Gongalong berry. To think I may never be silver again. All I have as a reminder of this magic show is the blue of your circus tent. Will I always be covered in it?"

"No," said Mr. Tiger. "The tent will shrink to its original size by the time you go to bed."

"Then I will wear it as a badge of honor," replied the magnificent moon.

The stars crowded closer to make sure the moon returned to its throne in the sky. Mr. Tiger felt there was no need to say any more. Betsy climbed onto his back, holding tight to the toad as they made their way down the ladder to where Ivan was waiting. The Gongalong band played the blues as they watched from below, as the moon, guided by the stars, was taken home.

·+· 22 ·+·

Dad and the Gongalongs were waiting. They wore dark glasses. Dad had insisted, as it was one of the three instructions.

"Best to be on the safe side," he had said.

All the would-be berry pickers held butterfly nets, in case Dad's machine didn't work. For there was no way of testing it. No one knew for certain what Gongalong berries looked like, or even how you harvested them.

Dad nearly missed noticing that the moon had turned blue. It was only when the leaves of the Gongalong bushes started to shimmer that he saw the reason for the dark glasses. The ripe berries shone as bright as gems. They looked more like jewels than fruit. Glimmering with the colors of the rainbow, they popped off the bushes and began to fly up toward the moon.

"What do we do?" shouted the Gongalong berry pickers, as they ran this way and that, bumping into one another and falling over themselves. The berries led them a merry dance and seemed to be getting away.

"Don't worry," said Dad, who was very worried as he cranked the handle of his machine. To calm himself he said his poem under his breath:

"This is my latest invention
It's made from an um
Which is found in an engine
With part of a drum
And a chain from my bike
Stuck together with . . ."

There was a moment's silence.
Then a loud clunk and a gurgling
sound, which went on longer than
a gurgling sound ever should.
Before the "um" of a sound
began to hum, there was

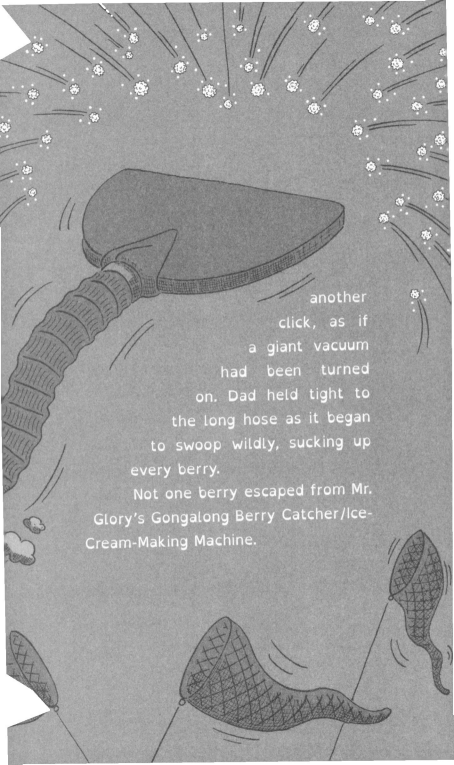

another
click, as if
a giant vacuum
had been turned
on. Dad held tight to
the long hose as it began
to swoop wildly, sucking up
every berry.

Not one berry escaped from Mr.
Glory's Gongalong Berry Catcher/Ice-
Cream-Making Machine.

By the time the sun had opened one eye on the new day, it would never have guessed where Mr. Tiger's circus had been. Though it did wonder what the moon was doing with a circus tent pinned to its silvery surface.

By ten in the morning, Mr. Alfonso Glory had made the ice cream. It was a multicolored confection that fizzed and frothed with glitter.

"Can I try some?" asked Betsy. "Please, oh, pretty please."

"No," said Dad. "There is just enough for the toad, the Gongalongs, and one scoop for Ivan. That's all. We don't need wishes, do we?"

"I suppose not," said Betsy. "Though I would like a brother or sister."

Dad laughed. "You don't have to

wish for that. Now help me hand out
the ice cream."

The toad was the first to be given
a scoop. She was sitting on a cushion
(a great improvement on the slimy
stone) with her legs crossed as her
tongue flicked out to roll a scoop of

ice cream into her mouth.

"What does it taste like?" Dad asked.

"It tastes of wishes, of raspberries and cream tea on hot summer days. Then slightly of lemon. Now of macaroons and cakes. Oh, how it fizzes on my tongue . . . then it . . ."

But before the toad could finish what she was trying to say, to everyone's amazement, she began to blow up. She

became bigger, even bigger than when she made her blue moon wish. Bigger and bigger, until . . . No one dared look in case she was going to explode. And explode she did, into a shower of rainbow colors.

Mr. Glory was terribly worried he might have killed the toad by mistake. As for the Gongalongs, they were weeping, wailing, and gnashing their teeth.

"Where has our princess gone?" they cried. "She was as delicate as china cups and strong as cement."

In the wailing and gnashing of teeth,
hardly anyone noticed when the
glitter cleared. Where once sat
the toad, now stood Princess Albee.
Twinkly, picture-pretty, delicate as
china cups, and as strong as cement.
On the turn of a sixpence, sadness
became joy.

"Our beloved princess is back," the
Gongalongs cried.

Princess Albee stuck out her tongue

and asked Betsy if it was still very long.

"No," said Betsy. "Not at all."

"And I do not look like a toad?"

"No, not at all."

"Not even a little bit?"

"No," said Betsy again.

The Gongalongs, seeing that the wish had worked, quickly lined up for a scoop of wishable ice cream. Dad, Betsy, and Mr. Tiger handed it out as fast as they could. In no time, wishes started to pop up right, left, and very much off center.

"The thing about wishes," Mr. Tiger said later, "is that very few people ever tell you what they would truly wish for."

So it came as a bit of a surprise when humble houses became palaces. Grand towers sprang up where once

there had been garden sheds. Balconies appeared from every upper-floor window, overlooking fountains and hanging gardens. There were houses shaped like ships and houses shaped like castles. In fact, a hodgepodge of dreams, the like of which you never have seen.

Mr. Tiger, Betsy, Dad, and Ivan, who was carrying Mum, stood, amazed by what they saw. Everything happened so fast, no one was quite sure who had wished for what.

"I think," said Betsy, looking at the town, "it looks like one of the most interesting places one would ever like to visit. On or off the map of the world."

Everyone agreed that it had been changed for the better. It was, thought Betsy, Christmas, birthdays, and happy-ever-afters wrapped together.

The ice cream had nearly gone; there was one scoop left for Ivan. He ate it slowly with his eyes tight shut. Everyone stood well back. Nothing happened. They waited and still nothing happened.

"What did you wish for?" asked Betsy.

Ivan said not a word.

"A house?" suggested Mr. Tiger.

"I didn't wish for a house," said Ivan glumly. "I wished to see my mum."

"Oh dear," said Betsy. "Perhaps she is busy."

Just then a door in the side of the mountain opened. A door no one knew was even in the side of the mountain. There stood a giant of a woman, in a coat, holding a handbag. "Ivan, my sunshine, how lovely to see you. Why, you have grown. Look at you, all smartly turned out."

"Mum," said Ivan.

She gave him a hug. "I've booked us a table at the Vine."

"You will be coming back, Ivan the Bold?" cried the Gongalongs. "We would be lost without you."

"Of course," said Ivan.

"Oh, for he's a jolly good top!" sang the Gongalongs.

"What did I tell you, son?" said his mum, as she closed the door in the mountain. "I knew you would do well and make your old mum proud."

·✦ 24 ✦·

The following night, Dad wheeled Mum in a wheelbarrow up to Princess Albee's palace. He was dressed in his best suit and Mum wore a sparkle gown, with glitter starfish in her hair. Betsy wore a dress made for her by the Gongalong costume designer. On her feet were gold, twinkly pointy shoes. The royal gardens were full of lights and tables of food, fireworks, and balloons.

There, under the moon and stars, the band played while Dad held Mum in his arms and whirled her round the dance floor. Betsy went and stood next to Mr. Tiger. Both looked down toward the harbor, over a town of wishes, where their ship was waiting. Soon they would be sailing home.

Betsy sighed. "I don't want this to end," she said.

"Ends," said Mr. Tiger, "are like goodbyes, and I don't do either." He took out his pocket watch.

"What can you see?" asked Betsy.

"I see, Betsy K. Glory, that this is just the beginning."

"Really?" she said, feeling a tingle

of excitement. "So it is not goodbye?"

"Not even halfway toward goodbye. You and I have many more adventures ahead of us. What do you say to that?" said Mr. Tiger.

"That sometimes I think happiness is a red balloon," said Betsy. "Round and big enough to lift you off your feet."

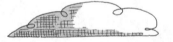

"It is indeed," said Mr. Tiger.

# FROG NOTE

Now we, the letters of the alphabet, have finished the story to the best of our abilities. We feel it's only fair and two corners square to tell you what happened to the frog, once known as Princess Olaf. She was taken to London Zoo. Being such a rare and special frog of unknown species, she had a new building built to house her. As well as a whole department of professors and researchers who spent their days observing her and writing learned works about her. Which were far too tricky for us, the letters of the alphabet, to understand.

Anyway, it bubbled down to the fact that she was unlike any other frog, on or off the map of the world. She soon forgot about being a princess and of ever having had a toad for a half sister. For here, at London Zoo, there was room service just like in her palaces. There was the finest grub a frog could eat, with a thousand vintages of pond water to choose from. But more important still, there was no other frog to outshine her. She was the one and only. Which, after all, is what she truly had wished for.

Crumble cakes!

# MR. TIGER, BETSY, AND THE SEA DRAGON
coming soon in Fall 2020

A wicked pirate captain and his crew are marauding in the seven seas near the island left off the map of the world. A very rare egg has gone missing and there is one unhappy sea dragon who wants it back. It's time for Mr. Tiger, Betsy, and the Gongalongs to set sail on their second adventure . . .

# AUTHOR'S NOTE

Ever since the publication of *I, Coriander*, I have been a passionate advocate for dyslexia being valued for what it is—the gift of creativity. In that pursuit I started NUword, a charity that takes a more optimistic view of this talent.

The educational system we have in place today, alas, manages to fail dyslexic children year upon year. We are wasting some of the greatest talent this country has to offer. For many dyslexic children, school is a nightmare to be endured. I look forward to the day when we let our young people take oral examinations, when we celebrate the diversity of their creative thinking and imagination.

If we don't, I believe we will lose those with the ability to think outside the box. Entrepreneurs, artists, writers and thinkers, scientists, mathematicians, judges, and many more who are part of our varied and amazing community.

*

I want to thank my editor and publisher, Fiona Kennedy. We've worked together on numerous books and she is, without doubt, one of my favorite editors of all time. It was she who cleverly found me Nick Maland. He has worked unbelievably hard and made this book into something quite magical, for which I thank him enormously. It has been a delight to work with Jessie Price and Clémence Jacquinet and all the enthusiastic, creative team that makes up Zephyr.

Last, but not least, thank you to my daughter, Freya Corry. I always need someone to help me get what I call a clean script. Freya was excellent at keeping me on track and coming up with some good ideas when mine seemed to wane.

Sally Gardner, Sussex, May 2018